TIM AND LUCY GO TO SEA

by
Edward Ardizzone

FRANCES LINCOLN CHILDREN'S BOOKS

First published by Oxford University Press in 1958
This edition published in Great Britain in 2005 and in the USA in 2006
by Frances Lincoln Children's Books, 4 Torriano Mews,
Torriano Avenue, London NW5 2RZ

www.franceslincoln.com

Distributed in the USA by Publishers Group West

British Library Cataloguing in Publication Data available on request

ISBN 1-84507-457-2

Printed in Belgium

1 3 5 7 9 8 6 4 2

Lucy Brown was a little girl seven years old. She lived with an old friend named Mr Grimes in his beautiful house in the country. She was very happy, but she sometimes wished she had another child to play with.

Now one day, as she was sitting on the garden wall, thinking and thinking, whom should she see trudging along the road but a small boy of about her own age? He was carrying a bundle and a stick.

"Hallo boy!" she said. "Where are you going and what is your name?"

"My name is Tim," answered the boy, "I am a sailor, and I have been shipwrecked. I am now looking for another ship."

Lucy was excited. Then she had an idea. "Come and see my guardian, Mr Grimes," she said. "Perhaps he will buy a steam yacht and then we can all go to sea."

Mr Grimes was delighted with the idea and asked Lucy to ring the bell for Mrs Smawley, his housekeeper, so that he could speak to her about it.

Alas, Mrs Smawley did not like the idea a bit. She said no, she was sure they would all be drowned, and, anyway, the sea always made her sick.

"Stuff and nonsense," said Mr Grimes.

"Order the car, we will go and look for a yacht at once."

Tim said that he knew of a steam yacht called *Evangeline* which was for sale at Portsmouth.

When they arrived at the harbour they all got into a small boat and Tim, with great skill, rowed them out to the yacht.

It was a beautiful yacht with a black hull, golden figurehead, red funnel, and yellow cabins on the deck.

Soon Tim had brought them alongside.
Lucy was the first up the gangway while
Tim, like a proper boatman, stayed behind
to help Mr Grimes and Mrs Smawley
disembark.

Mr Grimes was delighted with the yacht and said he would buy it. Mrs Smawley only sniffed, but you can imagine how excited Lucy was!

Tim was pleased too, and told Mr Grimes that he knew of a very good Captain and a very good cook.

"Good," said Mr Grimes, "send them a telegram telling them to come here at once. Oh, and by the way, tell the Captain to bring some sailors with him."

Tim went out and sent a telegram to the Captain, who was no other than the captain of the ship in which Tim had run away to sea. He also sent a telegram to the cook, who had also been on the ship and was a family man.

The next thing Mr Grimes did was to buy a lot of dark blue jerseys with *S.Y.Evangeline* printed on them for the crew.

He also bought two small ones for Tim and Lucy. They were very proud of them.

Early the next day the crew arrived on board the *Evangeline*.

Tim was pleased to see the Captain again and hurried to introduce him to Mr Grimes. They both liked each other at once.

Tim then introduced his old friend, the
cook, to Lucy, and then all three went below
to look at the galley.

The cook thought it was the best galley
he had ever seen.

That evening Tim and Lucy and the crew
went for a walk in the town, partly to have

a look round, but chiefly to show off their beautiful new jerseys.

For the next few days they were all very
busy getting the *Evangeline* ready for sea.
There were decks to be scrubbed,
painting to be done, and provisions to
be put on board.

Tim and Lucy helped with the painting. They enjoyed doing it very much, and became very good at it, and did not get any paint on their clothes.

Mr Grimes trotted about making suggestions and the Captain was busiest of all seeing that everything was done properly.

Mrs Smawley worked hard too, but she was sad.

When Mr Grimes asked her how she was enjoying herself, she said, "I know how to do my duty, sir. It is not for me to complain."

However, all the work was done at last, to the Captain's satisfaction and he reported to Mr Grimes that the ship was ready to sail on the morning tide.

How excited they all were!

Mr Grimes immediately had a conference with the Captain, and Tim and Lucy, who were listening at the door, heard such words as – Portugal – then the Azores – What about popping over to Pernambuco? – and so on.

Every face had a smile on it except one and that was Mrs Smawley's. She looked proud and sad as she stood by the after hatch staring at the shore.

It was a lovely day when the *Evangeline*, looking very smart in her new coat of paint and with all her flags flying, steamed out of the harbour for the open sea.

Tim and Lucy and Mr Grimes were on

deck. But Mrs Smawley went straight below and put herself
to bed.

This was the beginning of many happy days.

Lucy loved the life at sea, especially as she had Tim there to tell her about everything.

Also, she made great friends with the second mate, and used to tidy his cabin and darn his socks.

This pleased him very much, as he was a bachelor and very untidy.

Often Tim and Lucy would go to the galley. If the cook was busy they would help him with the cooking, but if he was free, he would sit down and tell them wonderful stories of his life at sea.

Mr Grimes was happy too, but Mrs Smawley became sadder and sadder and more and more sick, until Mr Grimes felt he had been unkind to make her come to sea with him.

At last Mr Grimes decided, for Mrs Smawley's sake, to turn back and make for home, especially as the sea was getting rather rough.

Then an adventure happened which made a great difference to all of them.

By now it was blowing a gale and the sea was really rough.

Tim was on the bridge with the Captain, when he saw, bobbing about among the great waves, a raft with some men on it.

"Tim," said the Captain, "we must rescue them. Call the second mate, tell him to get a boat's crew together and order all hands on deck to lower away a boat."

With great difficulty they managed to get a boat away.

In the meantime Mrs Smawley, hearing the noise and wondering what had happened, had hurried on deck.

At last, owing to the great bravery of the crew, all the men on the raft were saved; but they were a villainous looking lot and the Captain said he would be glad when they were put ashore.

Mrs Smawley, who was watching the

rescue, felt sure something terrible would happen, and something terrible nearly did happen.

A day or two later Tim and Lucy were going into the store room when they heard the rescued men plotting to capture the ship.

"Oh! What shall we do?" said Lucy.
"Hush," whispered Tim, "I have an idea."
He crept quietly forward, slammed the
door, and bolted it.

Then Tim and Lucy ran as fast as they could to the Captain.

"Quick," said the Captain, "to the forward hatch. They will try and escape that way."

But Mrs Smawley was on deck. She had heard the terrible shouts of the mutineers, when they had found that they were locked in, and was horrified to see the hatch cover slowly open and a head appear.

With great presence of mind she slammed down the hatch cover and sat on it.

In a moment, but only just in time, Tim and Lucy and the Captain arrived to help her hold it down.

The door and the hatch cover having
been secured by the crew, the Captain said
that, as the mutineers were desperate
characters and might escape, all able bodied
men in the ship must form an armed guard
and take it in turn to watch over them.

Mr Grimes said that he had once been a very good shot, and insisted on taking his turn with the others.

Tim shared the night watch with the cook.

Meanwhile, Mrs Smawley and Lucy busied themselves cooking food and brewing tea for the crew when they came off watch. Mrs Smawley was too excited and too busy to feel sick.

At last a warship was sighted. It had
come in answer to the Captain's S.O.S.
   All the crew were very relieved and gave
a great cheer when they heard the news.

Soon the warship was alongside. A party of Naval ratings came aboard the *Evangeline*, handcuffed the mutineers, and led them off in chains.

The Captain of the warship congratulated Tim and Lucy and Mrs Smawley on their bravery and presence of mind.

"Now!" said Mr Grimes, thinking again of poor Mrs Smawley. "Perhaps it is time we all went home."

"Oh please, sir," said Mrs Smawley, "don't go home for my sake. I like the sea now and don't feel sick any more."

"Bravo!" said Mr Grimes.

"Hurrah!" shouted Tim and Lucy.

"TIM," said Mr Grimes, "RUN AND TELL THE CAPTAIN TO MAKE FOR THE OPEN SEA!"

— *The End* —